Wm. W. Baskerville

Southern Writers

Biographical and critical studies

Wm. W. Baskerville

Southern Writers
Biographical and critical studies

ISBN/EAN: 9783337386429

Printed in Europe, USA, Canada, Australia, Japan

Cover: Foto ©Raphael Reischuk / pixelio.de

More available books at **www.hansebooks.com**

No. 1. Ten Cents.   Per Year, One Dollar.

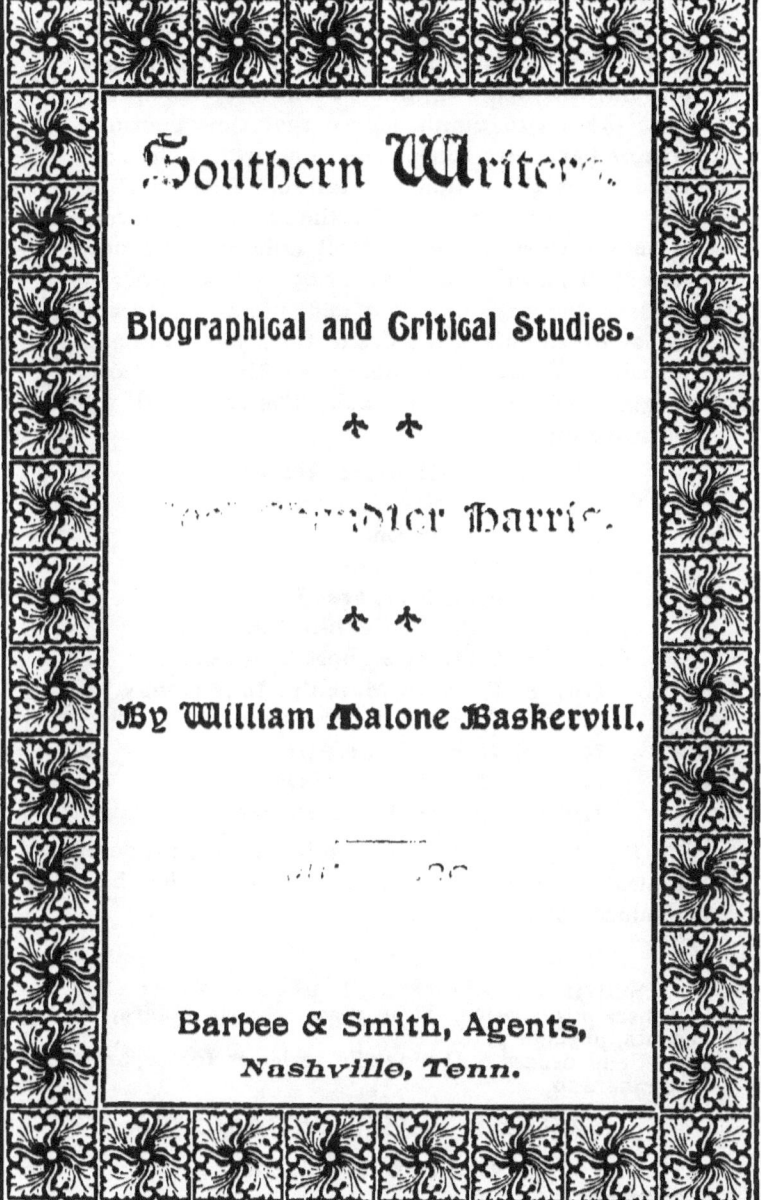

Southern Writers.

Biographical and Critical Studies.

✶ ✶

Joel Chandler Harris.

✶ ✶

By William Malone Baskervill.

Barbee & Smith, Agents,
Nashville, Tenn.

SOUTHERN WRITERS SERIES.

IN a series of twelve papers the writer proposes to give a tolerably complete survey of that literary movement which, beginning about 1870, has spread over the entire South. Since that time Southern writers have been conspicuous among the chief contributors to the nation's literature. There will be no attempt to place a final estimate upon this contribution, though some critical opinions will now and then be offered. The effort will be rather to present biographical *data* and literary appreciations—to stimulate the desire for a more intimate acquaintance with this literature which is so fresh, original, and racy of the soil. The series will appear as follows:

No. 1. Joel Chandler Harris.
No. 2. Maurice Thompson.
No. 3. Sidney Lanier.
No. 4. Irwin Russell.
No. 5. Mrs. Margaret J. Preston.
No. 6. George Washington Cable.
No. 7. Charles Egbert Craddock.
No. 8. Richard Malcolm Johnston.
No. 9. Thomas Nelson Page.
No. 10. James Lane Allen.
No. 11. Miss Grace King.
No. 12. Samuel Minturn Peck.

These writers may not unfairly be considered typical and representative of the best that has been produced in this new era.

SOUTHERN WRITERS: Published Monthly. Subscription price, $1 a year. Single copies, 10 cents, postage paid.
Send orders for the whole series or for separate numbers to

BARBEE & SMITH, Agents,
Nashville, Tenn.

Joel Chandler Harris.

MIDDLE GEORGIA is the birthplace and home of the raciest and most original kind of Southern humor. In this quarter native material was earliest recognized and first made use of. A school of writers arose who looked out of their eyes. and listened with their ears, who took frank interest in things for their own sake, and had enduring astonishment at the most common. They seized the warm and palpitating facts of everyday existence, and gave them to the world with all the accompaniments of quaint dialect, original humor, and Southern plantation life. The Middle Georgians are a simple, healthy, homogeneous folk, resembling for the most part other Southerners of like rank and calling in their manners, customs, and general

1

way of living. But they have developed a certain manly, vigorous, fearless independence of thought and action, and an ever increasing propensity to take a humorous view of life. In their earlier writings it is a homely wit, in which broad humor and loud laughter predominate; but tears are lurking in the corners of the eyes, and genuine sentiment nestles in the heart. In more recent times the horizon has widened, and there has been a gain in both breadth of view and depth of insight. Genius and art have combined to make this classic soil.

It is a small section of country, comprising only a few counties, but with them are indelibly associated the names of A. B. Longstreet, W. T. Thompson, J. J. Hooper, Francis O. Ticknor, Richard Malcolm Johnston, Harry Stillwell Edwards, Sidney Lanier, Maurice Thompson, Joel Chandler Harris, and many other less known writers. If we turn to their characters and scenes, the associa-

tion is still more intimate. Ransy
Sniffle and Ned Brace belong to
Baldwin, the scene of " The Fight,"
" The Gander Pulling," and " The
Militia Drill." In the woods and
along the river banks of the same
county " The Two Runaways "
were wont at a later day to enjoy
t h e i r annual escapade. " Simon
Suggs " was a native of Jasper;
" Major Jones's Courtship " took
place in Morgan; " Mr. Absalom
Billingslea and O t h e r Georgia
Folk " are at home in Hancock;
but to Putnam County was awarded
the honor of giving birth to " Uncle
Remus," a veritable E t h i o p i a n
Æsop, philosopher, and gentleman,
and to the " Little Boy," whose
inexhaustible curiosity and eager-
ness to hear a " story " have called
forth the most valuable and, in the
writer's opinion, the most perma-
nent contribution to American literature in the last quarter of this
century.

This school of humorists are not

realists at all in the modern sense; for nothing is farther from their writings than sadness, morbidness, and pessimism. Naturalism is the term by which their literary method may best be characterized. They look frankly and hearken attentively, following, at a great distance it ` may be, Fielding's and the great master's plan of holding the mirror up to nature. But coloring, tone, and substance have been reproduced with such absolute fidelity because the heart is full of hope, the eye bright, and a smile ever playing around the mouth. It is also easy to see that they are to the manner born. "To be sure," says Judge Longstreet, "in w r i t i n g the 'Georgia Scenes' I have not confined myself to strictly veracious historic detail; but there is scarcely one word from the beginning to the end of the book that is not strictly *Georgian*. The s c e n e s which I describe—as, for instance, 'The Gander Pulling'—occurred at

the very place where I locate them."
Shortly after the appearance of
" The Adventures of Capt. Simon
Suggs," a friend met the original
on the streets of Monticello and
said : " Squire Suggs, do you re-
member Jonce Hooper — little
Jonce?" " Seems to me I do,"
replied Mr. Suggs. " Well, Squire,
little Jonce has gone and noveled
you." Mr. Suggs looked serious.
" Gone and noveled me?" he ex-
claimed. " Well, I'll be danged!
Gone and noveled me? What
could 'a possessed him?" Since
the Civil War the " noveling"
process has gone on with enlarged
sympathies and greater success. A
new figure has been added to the
picture, making it more complete—
the negro. With the wider view
has also come greater freedom of
treatment, and no writers in the
South have appreciated this mental
and artistic liberty more than the
Georgians. Each of them has, by
means of the simplicity, humor, and

individuality which characterize the school, made a distinct contribution to the sum of human interest and enjoyment. But the most sympathetic, the most original, the truest delineator of this larger life—its manners, c u s t o m s, amusements, dialect, folklore, humor, pathos, and character—is Joel Chandler Harris.

His birthplace was Eatonton, the capital of Putnam County, in Middle Georgia, and the date of his birth December 9, 1848. S l i g h t biographical and personal sketches of him have appeared in the *Critic*, in *Literature*, and i n t h e *Book Buyer*, but the best account of his early life is to be found in "On the Plantation," one of the most interesting books that Mr. Harris has written. In this delightful volume it is not easy to tell "where confession ends and how far fiction embroiders truth." But the author has kindly left it to the reader to "sift the fact from the fiction, and label it to suit himself." As has been said of another romancer, it is not through the accidental circumstances of his life that he belongs to history, but through his talent; and his talent is in his books. Our first glimpse of Mr. Harris is in the little post office of Eatonton, which is also a "country store," and much frequented for both purposes. He is sitting upon a rickety, old, faded green sofa, in a corner of which he used to curl up nearly every day, reading such stray newspapers as he could lay his hands on, and watching the people come and go. His look betrays shyness and sensitiveness, though it is full of observation. He is reading in a Milledgeville paper the announcement of a Mr. Turner, whose acquaintance he has recently made, that he will begin the publication the following Tuesday of a weekly newspaper, to be called the *Countryman*. It is to be modeled after Mr. Addison's little paper, the *Spectator*, Mr. Goldsmith's little paper,

7

the *Bee*, and Mr. Johnson's little paper, the *Rambler*. He has heard of these, for he has had a few terms in the Eatonton Academy, and read some of the best books of the eighteenth century. When the " Vicar of Wakefield " is mentioned his eye sparkles, for since he was six years of age that wonderful story has been a stimulus to his imagination, and made him eager to read all books. He is proud of his acquaintance with a real editor, and waits with great impatience for the first issue of the *Countryman*. In the meanwhile we learn that he cannot be called a studious lad, or at any rate that he is not at all fond of the books in his desk at the Eatonton Academy. On the contrary, he is of an adventurous turn of mind, full of all sorts of pranks and capers; and plenty of people in the little town are ready to declare that he will come to some bad end if he is not more frequently dosed with what the old folks call " hickory oil." But he has a strange sympathy with animals of all kinds, especially horses and dogs, and a deeper, tenderer sympathy with all human beings.

At last the first issue arrives, and is read from beginning to end—advertisements and all. The most important thing in it, as it turned out, was the announcement that the editor wanted a boy to learn the printing business. The friendly postmaster furnished pen, ink, and paper, and the lad applied for the place and got it. Mr. Turner lived about nine miles from Eatonton, on a plantation of some two thousand acres, which was well supplied with slaves, horses, dogs, and game of different kinds. He was a lover of books, and had a choice collection of two or three thousand volumes. His wealth also enabled him to conduct the only country newspaper in the world, which he did so successfully that it reached a circulation of nearly two thousand copies. On the plantation was a pack of well-trained harriers, with which the little printer hunted rabbits, and a fine hound or two of the Birdsong breed, with which he chased the red fox. With the negroes he learned to hunt coons, and possums, and from them he heard those stories which have since placed their narrator in the list of the immortals. The printing office sat deep in a large grove of oaks, full of gray squirrels which kept the solitary typesetter company, running about over the roofs and playing "hide and seek" like children. From his window he watched the partridge and her mate build their artful nest, observed their coquetries, and from her mysteriously skillful manner of drawing one away from her nest or her young he learned one of his earliest and most puzzling lessons in bird craft. The noisy jay, the hammering woodpecker, and the vivacious and tuneful mocking bird lent their accompaniment to the clicking of the types. At twelve years of age, then, Mr. Harris found himself in this ideal situation for the richest and most healthful development of his talents. Type-setting came easy, and the lad had the dogs to himself in the late afternoon and the books at night, and he made the most of both. The scholarly planter turned him loose to browse at will in his library, only now and then giving a judicious hint. The great Elizabethans first caught his fancy, and quaint old meditative and poetical Sir Thomas Browne became one of his prime favorites, a place he yet holds. He made many friends among the standard authors that only a boy of a peculiar turn of mind would take to his bosom. But no book at any time has ever usurped the place of the inimitable " Vicar of Wake-field " in his affections—Goethe's, Scott's, Irving's, Thackeray's, all humanity's adorable Vicar. Mr. Harris, like Sir Walter, has read it in youth and in age, and the charm endures. In a recent paper he wrote: "The first book that ever attracted my attention, and the one that has held it longest, was and is the 'Vicar of Wakefield.' The only way to describe my experience with that book is to acknowledge that I am a crank. It touches me more deeply, it gives me the 'all-overs' more severely than all others. Its simplicity, its air of extreme wonderment, have touched and continue to touch me deeply." These two favorites have since that early period found worthy rivals in the Bible and Shakespeare, and he is specially serious when he talks of his heroes, Lee, Jackson, and Lincoln. Job, Ecclesiastes, and Paul's writings are his prime favorites; but all good books interest him more or less, though at the present time an ardent young writer on a pilgrimage to this shrine would perhaps find Mr. Harris's library as scantly supplied as Mr. Howells found Hawthorne's. There are only a few books, but they are the best, and they have been read and reread. Emerson, however, is not of this number; his "queer self-consciousness" and attitude of self-sufficiency have never appealed to him in any winning way. "You cannot expect an uncultured Georgia cracker to follow patiently the convolute diagrams of the oversoul," he will say; adding, with a quizzical smile: "You see I am perfectly frank in this, presenting the appearance of feeling as proud of my lack of taste and culture as a little girl is of her rag doll." But when culture and individuality are united, as he found them in Lowell, they receive his frankest admiration. "Culture is a very fine thing, indeed," he wrote of Mr. Lowell on his seventieth birthday, "but it is never of much account, either in life or in literature, unless it is used as a cat uses a mouse, as a source of mirth and luxury. It is at its finest in

13

this country when it is grafted on the sturdiness that has made the nation what it is, and when it is fortified by the strong common sense that has developed and preserved the republic. This is culture with a definite aim and purpose, . . . and we feel the ardent spirit of it in pretty much everything Mr. Lowell has written." As for the realists, he admires "immensely" what is best in them, though he has no fondness for minute psychological analysis. He likes a story and "human nature, humble, fascinating, plain, common human nature." "A man is known by the company he keeps," is a saying with a wider application, I fancy, than is comly given to it. I had a friend once —a strong, earnest, meditative, silent man—over the m a n t e l in whose study hung a portrait of William Cullen Bryant. The kinship of nature could easily be traced between these two and that great American of whom Bryant wrote:

The wildest storm that sweeps through
    space,
  And rends the oak with sudden force,
Can raise no ripple on his face,
  Or slacken his majestic course.

I could easily imagine my friend
in the heart of some primeval forest
—he had a deep and reverent love
of nature—repeating his favorite
lines :

    Be it ours to meditate,
In these calm shades, thy milder majesty,
And to the beautiful order of thy works
Learn to conform the order of our lives.

And so, consciously or unconscious-
ly, Mr. Harris has imbibed old-
fashioned ways of simplicity, naturalness, and truth from his Shakespeare and Bible ; has had ingrained
in the fiber of his being the gentle-
ness, delicacy, and purity of feeling
which distinguish the good Vicar's
author, and has conformed his life
to that sentiment of Sir Thomas
Browne's which "The Autocrat"
considered the most admirable in
any literature : "Every man truly
lives so long as he acts his nature

or some way makes good the faculties of himself."

Among these books he lived for several years, and almost before he knew it he was acquainted with those writers who lend wings to the creative imagination, if its delicate body has found habitation in a human soul. With the acquisition of knowledge went also hand in hand an observation of life and of nature. As he left his native village in the buggy with Mr. Turner, he had observed how quickly his little companions returned to their marbles after bidding him good-bye; and he had observed, too, how the high sheriff was "always in town talking politics," and talking "bigger than anybody." When he came to the plantation his observant eye took in everything, and the observations of the boy became the basis of the lifelong convictions and principles of the man. His greatest nature-gift, sympathy, put him in touch with dog and horse, with black runaway and white deserter, with the master and his slaves. These, he observed, treated him with more consideration than they showed to other white people, with the exception of their master. There was nothing they were not ready to do for him at any time of day or night. Taking him into their inner life, they poured a wealth of legendary folklore and story into his retentive ear, and to him revealed their true nature; for it is not a race that plays its tricks, as some one has said of nature, unreservedly before the eyes of everybody.

Mr. Harris has never had the slightest desire to become a man of letters; but the necessity of expressing himself in writing came upon him early in life. His first efforts appeared in the *Countryman*, sent in anonymously. Kindly notice and encouragement induced the young writer to throw off disguise and to write regularly. His contributions soon took a wider range, embracing local articles, essays, and poetry. But this idyllic existence was s u d d e n l y ended. Sherman's "march t h r o u g h Georgia" brought a corps of his army to the Turner plantation, and when the foragers departed they left little behind them except a changed order of things. The editor-planter called up those of his former slaves that remained, and told them that they were free. The *Countryman* passed away with the old order, devising, however, a rich legacy to the new. "A larger world beckoned [to the young writer] and he went out into it. And it came about that on every side he found loving hearts to comfort and strong and friendly hands to guide him. He found new associations, and formed new ties. In a humble way he made a name for himself, but the old plantation days still l i v e in his dreams." The "Wanderjahre" were few and un-

eventful. Now we find him setting
his "string" on the *Macon Daily
Telegraph*, then in a few months
he is in New Orleans as a private
secretary of the editor of the *Cres-
cent Monthly*, keeping his hand in,
however, by writing bright para-
graphs for the city papers. In a
short while he returns to Georgia to
become the editor of the *Forsyth
Advertiser*, one of the most influen-
tial weekly papers in the State. In
addition to the editorial work, he
set the type, worked off the edition
on a hand press, and wrapped and
directed his papers for the mail.
His bubbling humor and pungent
criticism of certain abuses in the
State were widely copied, and specially attracted the attention of Colo-
nel W. T. Thompson, the author
of "Major Jones's Courtship" and
other humorous books, who at that
time was editor of the *Savannah
Daily News*. He offered Mr. Harris a place on his staff, which was
accepted; and this pleasant associa-

tion lasted from 1871 to 1876. In the latter year a yellow fever epidemic drove him to Atlanta; he became at once a member of the editorial staff of the *Constitution,* and his literary activity began. And it is altogether fitting, too, that Mr. Harris's success should be identified with this popular journal, for no other newspaper published in the South has given so much attention to literary matters and encouragement to literary talent. Up to this time Mr. Harris had written, so far as I am aware, but one brief little sketch, a mere incident, which gave any promise of his future line of development and peculiar powers. It appeared in the *Countryman* at the close of the war—a little sequel to the passing of the Twentieth Army Corps, commanded by General Slocum, along the road by the Turner plantation. Thinking that the army would take another route, the lonely lad had seated himself on the fence, and before he knew it the troops were upon him. Their good-natured chaff he endured with a kind of stunned calmness till all passed. He then jumped from the fence and made his way home through the fields. "In a corner of the fence, not far from the road, Joe found an old negro woman shivering and moaning. Near her lay an old negro man, his shoulders covered with an old, ragged shawl. 'Who is that lying there?' asked Joe. 'It my ole man, suh.' 'What is the matter with him?' 'He dead, suh; but bless God, he died free!'"

Just before Mr. Harris went to Atlanta Mr. S. W. Small had begun to give the *Constitution* a more than local reputation by means of humorous negro dialect sketches. His resignation shortly afterwards made the proprietors turn for aid to Mr. Harris, who, taking an old negro whom he had known on the Turner plantation and making him chief spokesman, brought out in several sketches the contrast between the old and the new condition of things. But he soon tired of these, and one night he wrote the first sketch in " Legends of the Plantation," in which " Uncle Remus " initiates the " Little Boy," just as it now appears in his first published volume, entitled, " Uncle Remus : His Songs and Sayings." Fame came at once, though the invincible modesty of the author still refuses to recognize it. A number of things enhanced the value of this production—the wealth of folklore, the accurate and entertaining dialect, the delightful stories, the exquisite picture of " the dear remembered days." But the true secret of the power and value of " Uncle Remus " and his " Sayings " does not lie solely in the artistic and masterly setting and narration. The enduring quality lies there, for he has made a past civilization " remarkably striking to the mind's eye," and shown that rare ability " to seize the heart of the suggestion, and make a country famous with a legend." But underneath the art is the clear view of life, as well as humor, wit, philosophy, and "unadulterated human nature." We can get little idea of the revelation which Mr. Harris has made of negro life and character without comparing his conception and delineation with the ideal negro of "My Old Kentucky Home," "Uncle Tom's Cabin," and "Mars Chan" and "Meh Lady," and the impossible negro of the minstrel show. A few years ago the editor of the *Philadelphia Times* remarked that "it is doubtful whether the real negro can be got very clearly into literature except by way of minstrel shows and the comic drama." In answer to this Mr. Harris has truthfully said that "a representation of negro life and character has never been put upon the stage, nor anything remotely resembling it; but to all who have any knowledge of the negro, the plantation darky, as he was, is a very attractive figure. It is a silly trick of the clowns to give him over to burlesque, for his life, though abounding in humor, was concerned with all that the imagination of man has made pathetic." The negro of the minstrel show, black with burnt cork, sleek and saucy, white - eyed, red - lipped, crowned with plug hat, wearing enormous shoes, and carrying a banjo, rises to the dignity of a caricature only in the external appearance. The wit reeks with stale beer and the Bowery. Foster's " My Old Kentucky Home " is simply " Uncle Tom's Cabin " turned into a song ; and the latter, says Irwin Russell, " powerfully written as it is, gives no more true idea of negro life and character than one could get from the Nautical Almanac, and, like most other political documents, is quite the reverse of true in almost every respect." These contain the sentiments and the thoughts of artist-philanthropists belonging to a race " three or four thousand years in advance of them [the negroes] in mental capacity and moral force." They do breathe with infinite pathos the homely affection, the sorrows and hopes of everyday life, as these have been developed and conceived by the white race; but who ever heard that this was a favorite song or that a favorite book in any community of negroes? And so Mr. Page's "Marse Chan" and "Meh Lady," and Mr. Allen's "Two Gentlemen of Kentucky," are the answers of genius to genius and art pitted against art in this great controversy. In them the devotion, the doglike fidelity, and the unselfishness of the negro are used to intensify the pathos of the white man's situation, just as in the other case the pathos of the negro's situation was utilized to excite the philanthropy of the white man. In both cases the negro is a mere accessory, used to heighten the effect. It seems to be almost an impossibility for song writer, novelist, or serious historian to appreciate the nature or understand the condition of the plantation negroes; for otherwise, how can we account for so glaring a misconception as Mr. Bryce's, that they remained, up to the eve of emancipation, "in their notions and habits much what their ancestors were in the forests of the Niger or the Congo."

The Southern plantation negro sprang from the child race of humanity, and possessed only so much civilization as his contact with the white man gave him. Like children, he used smiles, cunning, deceit, duplicity, ingenuity, and all the other wiles by which the weaker seek to accommodate themselves to the stronger. Brer Rabbit was his hero, and " it is not virtue that triumphs, but helplessness; it is not malice, but mischievousness." In the course of time he became remarkable for both inherent and grafted qualities. Gratitude he was distinguished for; hospitality and helpfulness were his natural creed; brutality was conspicuously absent, considering the prodigious depth of his previous degradation. He did not lack courage, industry, self-denial, or virtue. He did an immense amount of quiet thinking, and, with only such forms of expression as his circumstances furnished, he indulged in paradox, hyperbole, aphorism, sententious comparison, and humor. He treasured his traditions, was enthusiastic, patient, long-suffering, religious, reverent. "Is there not poetry in the character?" asked Irwin Russell, the first, perhaps, to conceive and to delineate it with real fidelity to life. Since his all too untimely taking off many have attempted this subject; but no one has equaled the creator of "Uncle Remus," one of the very few creations of American writers worthy of a place in the gallery of the immortals; and he should be hung in the corner with such gentlemen as Col. Newcome and Sir Roger de Coverley, and not very far from Rip Van Win-

kle, my Uncle Toby, and Jack Fal-
staff.

Before the war Uncle Remus had
always exercised authority over his
fellow-servants. He had been the
captain of the corn pile, the stoutest
at the log rolling, the swiftest with
the hoe, the neatest with the plow,
the leader of the plantation hands.
Now he is an old man whose tall
figure and venerable appearance are
picturesque in the extreme, but he
moves and speaks with the vigor of
perennial youth. He is the embod-
iment of the quaint and homely humor, the picturesque sensitiveness—
a curious exaltation of mind and
temperament not to be defined by
words—and the really poetic imagination of the negro race; and over
all is diffused the genuine flavor of
the old plantation. With the art to
conceal art, the anthor retires behind
the scenes and lets this patriarch re-
veal negro life and character to the
world. Now it is under the guise
of Brer Rabbit, after his perilous

adventure with the tar baby and narrow escape from Brer Fox as he is seen "settin' cross-legged on a chinkapin log koamin' de pitch outen his har wid a chip," and "flingin' back some er his sass, 'Bred and bawn in a brier patch, Brer Fox; bred and bawn in a brier patch!'" Another phase is seen in "Why Brer Possum Loves Peace," a story of indolent good nature, questionable valor, and nonsensical wisdom: "I don' min' fightin' no mo' dan you doz, sez'ee, but I declar' to grashus ef I kin stan' ticklin.' An' down ter dis day," continued Uncle Remus, "down ter dis day, Brer Possum's boun' ter s'render w'en you tech him in de short ribs, en he'll laff ef he knows he's gwine ter be smashed for it." This whimsical defense of inborn cowardice has a touch of nature in it which makes it marvelously akin to Sir John's counterfeiting on Shrewsbury plain. But the prevailing interest is centered in Brer Rabbit's skill in outwitting Brer

Fox and the other animals, which is managed with such cleverness and good nature that we cannot but sympathize with the hero, in spite of his utter lack of conscience or conviction. But the chief merit of these stories, as Mr. Page has remarked, springs directly from the fact that Uncle Remus knows them, is relating them, and is vivifying them with his own quaintness and humor, and is impressing us in every phase with his own delightful and lovable personality. Mr. Harris's skill in narrative is well-nigh perfect, and the conversation, in which his books abound, is carried on with absolute naturalness and fidelity to life. The habit of thought as well as of speech is strikingly reproduced. Not a word strikes a false note, not a scene or incident is out of keeping with the spirit of the life presented. No one has more perfectly preserved some of the most important traits of Southern character, nor more enchantingly presented some of the most beau-

tiful phases of Southern civilization.

Other phases of negro character,
very different from those presented in
the "Legends," appeared in the "Sayings" and in various "Sketches,"
which reproduce "the shrewd ob-
ervations, the curious retorts, the
homely thrusts, the quaint com-
ments, and the humorous philosophy
of the race of which Uncle Remus
is a type." But in "Nights with
Uncle Remus," "Daddy Jake the
Runaway," and "Uncle Remus and
His Friends" we returned again to
the old plantation home; "daddy,"
"mammy," and the "field hands"
lived once more with their happy,
smiling faces; songs floated out upon
the summer air, laden with the per-
fume of rose and honeysuckle and
peach blossom, and mingled with
the rollicking medley of the mocking bird; and we felt that somehow
over the whole life the spell of genius had been thrown, rendering it
immortal. But it is with and through

the negro that Mr. Harris has wrought this wonder, for as Mr. Page says : "No man who has ever written has known one-tenth part about the negro that Mr. Harris knows, and for those who hereafter shall wish to find not merely the words, but the real language of the negro of that section, and the habits of mind of all American negroes of the old time, his works will prove the best thesaurus."

Again a larger world beckoned to the writer, as to the boy, and he entered the field of original story-telling and wider creative ability with perfect poise and consummate literary art in " Mingo," a " Cracker " tragedy, disclosing the pent-up rage of a century against aristocratic neighbors, antipathy to the negro, narrowness and pride, happily turned by Mingo's gratitude and watchful and protecting love for his young " Mistiss's " fatherless and motherless little girl into a smiling comedy, closing with this pretty picture:

"The sunshine falling gently upon his gray hairs, and the little girl clinging to his hand and daintily throwing kisses." Mingo, drawn with genuine sympathy and true skill, is one of the author's master-pieces; but we are somehow specially attracted to Mrs. Feratia Bivins, whose "pa would 'a' bin a rich man, an' 'a' owned *niggers*, if it hadn't but 'a' bin bekase he sot his head agin stintin' of his stomach," and whose sharp tongue, homely wit, and indignant hate portray the first of a group of the Mrs. Poyser-like women who give spice as well as life to the author's pages. Another is Mrs. Kendrick in "Blue Dave "—of which, by the bye, the author says, "I like 'Blue Dave' better than all the rest, which is another way of saying that it is far from the best "—whose humor conceals her own emotions, and flashes a calcium light upon the weaknesses of others. " Well, well, well!" said Mrs. Kendrick, speaking of the quiet, self-contained, elegant, and rather prim Mrs. Denham. " She always put me in mind of a ghost that can't be laid on account of its pride. But we're what the Lord made us, I reckon, and people deceive their looks. My old turkey gobbler is harmless as a hound puppy, but I reckon he'd bust if he didn't up and strut when strangers are in the front porch." " Uncle Remus," " Mingo," " Blue Dave," and " Balaam " belong to the class which " has nothing but pleasant memories of the discipline of slavery, and which has all the prejudices of caste and pride of family that were the natural results of the system." But " Free Joe " presents another phase—this heart tragedy brought about by the inhumanity of man and the pitiless force of circumstances. Nowhere has the helpless wretchedness of the dark side of slavery been more clearly recognized or more powerfully depicted. Truth demands that the complete picture shall be given, though silly scribbler or narrow bigot may accuse the author of trying to cater to Northern sentiment. Every now and then some Southern writer is subjected to this unmanly and ignoble insult, though much less frequently than formerly. Mr. Maurice Thompson's poem and Mr. Henry Watterson's speech on "Lincoln," Mr. James Lane Allen's lecture on "The South in Fiction," and Mr. W. P. Trent's "Life of William Gilmore Simms," seem to produce a mild form of rabies in certain quarters. "What does it matter," asks Mr. Harris, "whether I am Northern or Southern, if I am true to truth, and true to that larger truth, my own true self? My idea is that truth is more important than sectionalism, and that literature that can be labeled Northern, Southern, Western, or Eastern is not worth labeling at all." Shutting one's eyes to facts removes them neither from life nor from history. And so we are specially thankful to Mr. Harris for

" Free Joe," " Little Compton," and
all those passages in " On the Plantation " and his other writings which
lead us to a truer and larger humanity. His skillful manner of convey-
ing a lesson is admirably done at the
close of " Free Joe." This " black
atom drifting hither and thither without an owner, blown about by all the
winds of circumstance, and given
over to shiftlessness," is the person-
ification of helpless suffering, and
yet he chuckles as he slips away
from the cabin of the cracker broth-
er and sister into the night. Micajah
Staley, however, the representative
of too large a number, says : " Look
at that nigger; look at 'im. He's
pine blank as happy now as a kildee
by a mill race. You can't 'faze 'em.
I'd in about give up my t'other hand
ef I could stan' flat-footed an' grin
at trouble like that there nigger."
" Niggers is niggers," said Miss
Becky, smiling grimly, " an' you
can't rub it out; yit I lay I've seed
a heap of white folks lots meaner'n

Free Joe. He grins—and that's nigger—but I've ketched his underjaw a trimblin' when Lucindy's name uz brung up." He was found dead the next morning, with a smile on his face. "It was as if he had bowed and smiled when death stood before him, humble to the last." The world could ill spare woman's or the artist's eye.

Other stories, as "At Teague Poteet's," "Trouble on Lost Mountain," and "Azalia," show a steady gain in the range of Mr. Harris's creative power. The keenest interest was awakened when the first part of "At Teague Poteet's" came out in the *Century*, May, 1883, and the reader who happened to turn to the *Atlantic* for the same month and read "The Harnt That Walks Chilhowee" must have been surprised at the revelation which these two admirable stories made of the real and potent romance of the mountains and valleys of Tennessee and Georgia. This was a longer and more sustained effort than Uncle

Remus had ever attempted. It evinced an eye for local color, appreciation of individual characteristics, and the ability to catch the spirit of a people that could be as open as their valleys or as rugged, enigmatical, and silent as their mountains. Scene and character were vividly real, and the story was told with consummate art and unflagging interest till the climax was reached. "Trouble on Lost Mountain" sustained his reputation as a story-teller and added the element of tragic power.

At a first glance it would seem that these, with his previous writings, give promise of the fully developed novel with the old plantation life for a background and the nation for its scope. But it must not be forgotten that Mr. Harris is a hard-working journalist, seldom missing a day from his desk; and as Mr. Stedman has pointed out in regard to Bayard Taylor, "this task of daily writing for the press, while a good staff, is a poor crutch; it diffuses the heat of authorship, checks idealism, retards the construction of masterpieces." It is perhaps due to this that the love element in these stories lacks that romantic fervor and tenderness which make all the world love a lover. They are vivid and dramatic, sparkling with humor and keen observations, and revealing intimate knowledge of human hearts. But in "Azalia," for instance, the Southern general and his mother are rather conventional, and Miss Hallie is insipid, though through them we do catch glimpses of old Southern mansions, with their stately yet simple architecture, admirably illustrative of the lives and characters of the owners, and of the unaffected, warm, and gracious old-time hospitality. The Northern ladies, too, admirably described as they are in a few words, are slight sketches rather than true presentments. This story is particularly rich in types, but the real life in its humor and its pathos is in the "characters." Mrs. Haley, a lineal descendant of Mrs. Poyser; William, a little imp of sable hue that might serve as a weather-stained statue of comedy, if he were not so instinct with life; and Emma Jane Stucky —the representative of that indescribable class of people known as the piny woods "Tackies"—whose "pale, unhealthy-looking face, with sunken eyes, high check-bones, and thin lips that seemed never to have troubled themselves to smile — a burnt-out face that had apparently surrendered to the past and had no hope for the future"—remains indelibly etched upon the memory, making its mute appeal for human sympathy and helpful and generous pity. Like all genuine humorists, Mr. Harris has his wit always seasoned with love, and a moral purpose underlies all his writings. In the twelve volumes or more which he has published he has preserved traditions and legends, photographed a

civilization, perpetuated types, cre-
ated one character. Humor and sympathy are his chief qualities, and in
everything he is simple and natural.
Human character is stripped of tire-
less details. The people speak their
natural language, and act out their
little tragedies and comedies accord-
ing to their nature. " We see them,
share their joys and griefs, laugh at
their humor, and in the midst of all,
behold, we are taught the lesson of
honesty, justice, and mercy."

In person Joel Chandler Harris is
somewhat under the middle height,
compact, broad of shoulder, and rather rotund about the waist. But he
is supple, energetic, and his swing-
ing stride still tells of the freedom
which the boy enjoyed on the Turner plantation. He is the most pro-
nounced of blondes, with chestnut
hair, a mustache of the same color,
and sympathetic, laughing blue eyes.
Sick or well, he is always in a good
humor, and enjoys his work, his
friends, and his family. Sprung

from a simple, sincere race whose wants were few and whose tastes were easily satisfied, he is very honest and outspoken in his opinions and convictions, and the whole nature of the man tends to earnestness, simplicity, and truth. " I like people," he says, " who are what they are, and are not all the time trying to be what somebody else has been." In spite of the fame which has come unbidden, he still delights to luxuriate in the quiet restfulness of his semirural home in the little suburb of West End, three miles from the heart of Atlanta ; and we confess that we like best to think of him, as Mr. Brainerd once described him in the *Critic*, in this typical Southern cottage nestling in a grove of sweet gum and pine, enlivened by the singing of a family of mocking birds that wintered in his garden—and not a bird among them, we imagined, with whose peculiarities he was not familiar. In a distant corner of his inclosure a group of brown-eyed

Jerseys grazed. Hives of bees were placed near a flower garden that sloped down to the bubbling spring at the foot of the road, a few rods distant. The casual visitor, we were told, was apt to be eyed by the dignified glance of a superb English mastiff, followed by the bark of two of the finest dogs in the country—one a bull dog, the other a white English bull terrier. But this was published in 1885, and now Mr. Garsney, in the *Book Buyer* for March, 1896, tells us that the " grove of sweet gums," the " babbling brook," and the " droning bees are all fictions of somebody else's poetic fancy." Still Mr. Garsney, in his setting for the author of " Uncle Remus," has the eye of an artist and is himself full of poetry, however ruthless he may be with " poetic fancies," for after placing him " amid his roses," he adds : " The roses are his one passion, and under his tender care the garden—the finest rose garden in Atlanta outside of a

43

florist's domain—blooms with prodigal beauty from May until the middle of December. In the early summer mornings, when the mocking birds are trying their notes in the cedar, and the wrens are chirping over their nest in the old mail box at the gate, you can hear the snipping of the pruning shears, and you know that Joel Chandler Harris is caressing his roses while the dew is yet on their healthy leaves."

In this home, with its spacious verandas, generous hearths, and wide, sunny windows, the right man is sure to find a welcome. The house is one in which bric-a-brac, trumpery, and literary litter are conspicuously absent, but evidently a home where wife and children take the place of these inanimate objects of devotion. But here the man Joel Chandler Harris, as Carlyle would have said, is seen at his best. It is here that the usually silent or monosyllabic figure takes on life and shares with another his inner wealth of thought and fancy. Mr. Garsney, who had the good fortune to be an inmate of this home for some months, and to whose sketch the writer is indebted for many of these personal remarks and observations, thus describes certain rare moments: " It is in the darkness of a summer evening, on the great front porch of his house, or by his fireside, with no light save that from the flickering coals which he loves to punch and caress, that the man breaks forth into conversation. I have had in these rare twilight hours the plot of a whole book unfolded to me—a book that is yet in the dim future, but which will make a stir when it appears; I have heard stories innumerable of old plantation life and of happenings in Georgia during the war; and I have heard through the mouth of this taciturn and unliterary-looking man more thrilling stories of colonial life in the South than I had believed the South held. At these times the slight hesitancy that is usually apparent in his speech disappears; his thoughts take words and come forth, tinged by the quaint Georgia dialect, in so original a shape and so full of human nature that one remembers these hours long afterwards as times to be marked with a white stone."

But it is only to the chosen companion that he thus unlocks his treasures. He seldom has more than a word for ordinary acquaintances, and the ubiquitous interviewer he avoids as a deadly plague. From him the autograph fiends get no response, and many amusing stories are told of his success in eluding sightseers and lion-hunters. No inducement has yet prevailed upon him to appear in public, either as a reader or as a lecturer. "I would not do it for $1,-000,000," was once his response to an invitation to lecture. Many positions of great trust and prominence, we are told, have been refused by him, for he says: "If the greatest position on the round earth were to be offered me, I wouldn't take it. The responsibility would kill me in two weeks. Now I haven't any care or any troubles, and I have resolved never to worry any more. Life is all a joke to me. Why make it a care?"

To those who are engaged in the pigmy contests for money and place this philosophy will doubtless appear tame and unheroic. But for a man of Mr. Harris's peculiar gifts and temperament it is the highest wisdom. It means the saving for mankind what a few would squander upon themselves. It means more inimitable stories, and since his success in the past justifies us in expecting it, and especially since he has reached the age of ripest wisdom and supremest effort on the part of genius, it means, we may hope, a work into which he will put the wealth of his mind and heart, and expand and compress into one

47

---

novel the completest expression of his whole being. But if he should never give us a masterpiece of fiction like his beloved " Vicar of Wakefield," " Ivanhoe," " Vanity Fair," or " The Scarlet Letter," we shall still be forever grateful for the fresh and beautiful stories, the delightful humor, the genial, manly philosophy, and the wise and witty sayings in which his writings abound. His characters have become world possessions; his words are in all our mouths. By virtue of these gifts he will be enrolled in that small but distinguished company of humorists, the immortals of the heart and home, whose genius, wisdom, and charity keep fresh and sweet the springs of life, and Uncle Remus will live always.

Eminent Methodists.

SERIES FOR 1896.

THIS is a series of booklets, uniform in style with "Southern Writers," which is issued monthly. It will embrace twelve biographical sketches of eminent Methodists, written by Bishops O. P. Fitzgerald and Charles B. Galloway. The names of these distinguished authors give a pledge of the highest excellence, and we bespeak for the series a wide circulation. They will include the following:

Lovick Pierce,	George F. Pierce,
L. C. Garland,	Jefferson Hamilton,
Moses Brock,	Susanna Wesley,
H. N. McTyeire,	William Winans,
Robert A. Smith,	Benjamin M. Drake,
Robert Alexander,	James A. Duncan.

The first six numbers are already published, and the succeeding titles will follow monthly.

Subscription for the Whole Series, 50c.
Single Numbers, ... 5c.

———

Barbee & Smith, Agents,
NASHVILLE, TENN.

Writings of

Joel Chandler Harris

❧ ❧ ❧

Uncle Remus: His Songs and His Sayings. The Folklore of the Old Plantation. Illustrated........$2 00

Uncle Remus and His Friends. Old Plantation Stories, Songs, and Ballads, with Sketches of Negro Character. Illustrated. 1 50

Nights with Uncle Remus. Illustrated......................... 1 50

Mingo and Other Sketches in Black and White 1 25

Balaam and His Masters, and Other Sketches and Stories........... 1 25

Little Mr. Thimblefinger and His Queer Country. What the Children Saw and Heard There. Illustrated....................... 2 00

Mr. Rabbit at Home: A Sequel to Little Mr. Thimblefinger 2 00

On the Old Plantation. With Numerous Illustrations 1 50

❧ ❧ ❧

Barbee & Smith, Agents.

NASHVILLE, TENN.